How I CAN
Have Everything!

John Wolcott Adams

Published by Golden Key Publications
P. O. Box 30989
Phoenix, AZ 85046-0989 USA

Books by John Wolcott Adams

Positively Alive!
BE What You Are: LOVE
How to Have 'Unexpected' Income
Power Words for Prosperous Living!
Thirty Days to a Better Life!
How *I CAN* Have Everything!
Pro$per Now!
Life Is Choice

Cover Design and Photograph by John Wolcott Adams

ISBN-0-9602166-6-9
Library of Congress Control Number: 2003096360

Printed in the UNITED STATES OF AMERICA
10 9 8 7 6 5 4 3 2 1

Contents . . . .

Dedication

This book is lovingly dedicated to Victoria Benoit, a delightfully positive lady; a most loving, resonating, and helpful soul. Thank you, Victoria, for being you. And, to the memory of Doris Wolcott Jones, a favorite aunt who, early in my life, encouraged me to do what I am here to do, and helped to convince me that I Can.

Acknowledgments

Many thanks to *Charlotte Rogers Brown who so lovingly edited this book, to my Prayer Partners, and to all the charming people who lovingly help me in every way; for the teachings of Charles and Myrtle Fillmore, and for Emmet Fox, who, through his books, was one of my mentors. Thank you to all the wonderful people who read, are inspired, and are helped by my books.

*Charlotte Rogers Brown is co-author of, *A Weaving Of Wonder*, a wonderful book of fables for ALL ages. This inspiring book is good reading, and carries profound messages for all who have the privilege of reading *A Weaving Of Wonder*. Also, *In Our Shoes - Seven Women Reveal Their Soles*. Visit: www.Wonder-Weavers.com

Introduction

This is a lo-tech book. With all the hi-tech stuff we have today—the Internet and every electronic gadget imaginable—the tools contained in this book may sound deceptively simple. Yet for as wonderful as our electronic marvels can be, many people still have difficulty getting what they really want. Even with its vast sources of information and goods, the information highway cannot supply most desires of the heart, those that truly satisfy the soul.

You don't need sophisticated state-of-the-art electronic equipment to achieve what is really important to you. Even if you are a computer whiz or depend on electronics to earn a living, this book can help you get more of what you want.

Some of the best things in life come in simple ways—the simpler, the better. Too often we get caught up in complicated, complex ways of solving problems and achieving our goals. That is why I offer this lo-tech, simple, practical, and *easy* way of achieving what's really important. Your mind, imagination, and faith are all you need to make it work

You CAN have what you really, really desire, and a lot more! Whatever your heart desires is, in truth, already yours. You need only to learn how to claim, receive and experience it. This book gives you the keys for doing that.

In this book you will find a simple, practical tool to make your dreams come true. You will also find tips for using this tool and some inspiring success stories. Little did I realize when I first used this tool what a difference it would make in my life.

As it has been with all of my books, my intention in writing *How I CAN Have Everything!* is to empower you to have your heart's desires, more easily, without the usual strain and struggle.

You CAN have the love, peace, success, health, wealth, and happiness you desire. Let this book help you. Let it empower you to set free the "imprisoned splendor" within you; to reach for the stars and beyond; to achieve the seemingly impossible; to delight and fill your soul with ecstasy.

Never underestimate your self-worth. So many people do, keeping themselves from claiming the vast good God has for them. I urge you not to settle for less than the best of God's rich abundance. There is plenty for you, for everyone. If you are enjoying a substantial degree of success and prosperity, that is great! But are you as happy and healthy as you really can be? Do you have peace of mind? Do you love people and do people love you? Are you surrounded by beauty? Are you relaxed, healthy and free?

You are meant to have balance in all areas of your life. You are meant to be prosperous *and* happy, to be successful *and* have peace of mind, to be fulfilled *and* loved. God did not put you here to have half a loaf. He wants you to have it all.

If there is anything lacking in any area of your life, you can do something about it. It is essential to have an open mind, but real changes are made through the heart. Open your mind *and* heart to what is shared with you on these pages. Open your heart and allow yourself to learn as you did as a child. You will be amazed at the results! *Go for it with all your heart!*

John Wolcott Adams
P. O. Box 30989
Phoenix, AZ 85046-0989 USA

Prayer changes consciousness.
Consciousness changes the world.
-- Rev. Richard Rogers

1

There is no limit.
You CAN have everything!

The tool I share with you in this book appeared in my life just when I needed it most. It was in the mid-sixties, and I was struggling to create a new Unity church in Port Angeles, Washington. The "experts" said it couldn't be done; it had never been done in a town of only 15,000 people. However, the need was apparent, and I had the desire and determination to do something worthwhile. It was a pioneering effort that laid the groundwork for establishing Unity churches in many cities of that size and even smaller.

Although I was a new minister, I drew upon my inner resources of courage, spiritual potential and training. To help when times got tough, I made myself an "Eye CAN"—a simple tin can decorated with a photograph of an eye clipped from a magazine. It not only served as a tangible reminder of the inner resources always available to me, but as a container for all my growing beliefs and affirmations.

Real joy comes not from ease or riches
or from praise of others,
but from doing something worthwhile.
-- Sir Winfield Grenfell

I persisted until the church was established and it was time to move on and let others take it further. I persisted through many difficulties, even when there appeared to be no way. Now more than 30 years later, the church remains a source of positive inspiration for the people who live on the Olympic Peninsula along the beautiful shores of the Strait of Juan de Fuca. I am thankful for the members and friends who shared my dream and helped establish that church, and for the dedicated ministers who have carried on that ministry. We've all spent a lot of time in prayer. The church is there because of the Eye CAN and the steps I will share with you throughout this book. It's amazing how empowering the Eye CAN is!

There is absolutely no limit to what you can achieve when you take hold of the right idea with your mind and proceed with the right attitude. When you set your goals high, know the power of true achievement, and act on your ideas and beliefs without wavering, you are invincible. You are already successful in accomplishing the "impossible."

The Eye CAN is instantly effective and never fails to light up the lives of all who use it. Follow the steps outlined on these pages and you, too, will achieve greater degrees of happiness, prosperity, health, peace of mind,

*The eyes brighten with friendliness
and good cheer when animated by the
light of love, joy, faith or noble purpose.*

-- -- *Ernest Holmes*

and success. You will upgrade your faith. You will experience more love and courage while getting rid of old doubts, fears and stumbling blocks. You will create a better, more likeable, and more productive self-image.

You may experience the healing of an old condition that was once declared "incurable." But there is no such condition, because *with God all things are possible*. The only way a condition can be "incurable" is if we accept it as so, and resign ourselves to that conclusion—if we make up our minds and refuse to change.

How sad that so many people resign themselves to a fate someone else—a doctor, parent, boss, news anchor, or public official—has pronounced for them. Their word doesn't make something true; it is your decision whether or not to accept it as true.

There is no situation that cannot be corrected, no trouble so difficult that there cannot be found a satisfying solution. It may take time, but it *can* be found. Regardless of your condition—poor health, poor finances, unhappiness—you *can* rise into healthy, happy, prosperous living. You *can* when you dare to act. Even if you enjoy a wonderful level of prosperity, you can move on to even higher levels. There are no limits to the riches

Develop your own vision.
Define your dreams.
Set your goal.
Work out your action plan.
Develop the right habits.
Then just do it!
              -- Dexter R. Yoger, Sr.

of God, except for those limits you place upon yourself. Everything is possible for you, because you are one with the Spirit of God. Your good is unlimited because God is unlimited, and God is your ever-present resource. You need only to back up your belief with action.

It is really up to you. You CAN have everything!

We were born to make manifest the glory of God that is within us. It's not just in some of us, It's in everyone.
— Marianne Williamson

*Let us free ourselves and decide today
to be the real self that we are created to be.
Take time to discover your own wonderful
and special talent.
Refuse to see obstacles to succeed in living
a full, creative and prosperous life.
Say: I can succeed in a fabulous way!
Say it over and over and follow through
to success.*   -- *Amalie H. Frank

*From the book, *Amalie's Good Words -- Signposts for the Journey*
by Amalie H. Frank. Used by permission. Available from Rob & Bobbie
Brammer, 8266 Rivera Way, Port St. Louis, FL 34986

2

The Power of "I CAN"

How many people, after being told they would never walk again, have walked simply because they believed they could and made up their minds to do so? Helen Keller, who was blind and deaf, accomplished amazing things because of her basic "I can" attitude. The Wright brothers went ahead and flew their airplane, even when doubters said it couldn't be done. While they were scoffing, the Wright brothers were flying!

Quite a number of years ago, I knew a fellow who walked into a Cadillac dealership, decided on the Cadillac he wanted, ordered it, then paid only $500 down, saying he would be back in three months with the rest of the money to pick up his new car. Although the people in the dealership had placed little faith in his ability to fulfill his obligation and keep his $500 down payment, he kept his promise to the salesman and to himself. He simply kept telling himself, "I can," and worked like everything to prove that he could. With his "I can" attitude, he knew he couldn't fail.

*Your biggest weakness can be your
biggest strength and your greatest
challenge can become your greatest triumph.*
-- Dr. Delia Sellers*
(Getting It Right This Time)

*Dr. Delia Sellers, Abundant Living, P. O. Box 12525,
Prescott, AZ 86304 USA

Another man proved his doctors wrong by refusing to die when they said he would. After giving thought to the prospect of dying, he decided that living was better, so he chose to live. He kept saying to himself, "I can live, and I will!" And live he did, even though he had gone through three serious operations in a relatively short time.

Richard Rogers, senior minister of Unity Church of Phoenix, tells this story of how the power of "I can" worked in his life:

> While hiking in Colorado, I had this idea: What if I hiked all the way over the Continental Divide, from the last lake on the eastern side to the first lake on the western side? As soon as I thought of doing it, all the reasons for not doing it began to fill my mind. "It's too far. How will I get back? What if a lightning storm comes up?" Finally the voice within me said, "I can do this."
>
> As the day of the hike got closer, I had all the feelings again, and I asked myself, "Why am I doing this?" Again, the voice within me said, "Because I can." I wondered: How many other things had I not given myself permission to try? How many other mountain ranges had I wanted to hike, but talked myself out of? How many times had I played it safe?

My friend is one whom I can associate with my choicest thoughts.
-- Henry David Thoreau

The actual hike was long, hard, uncomfortable and, at times, scary. But I did it. I had a wonderful sense of accomplishment. I had set a goal and tested myself. I decided I would spend more time doing the things I can, while I can.

What is the power of "I can"? What is it that makes those words so potent? It is really quite simple, yet many people fail to see it. When you look at these words from a higher point of view, God's point of view, you realize that they contain great spiritual power to set free your inner resources. Speak these two words several times and be aware of how you feel when you say them. There is great mystical power contained in these two very short words.

The important thing to remember is that, of yourself alone, you can do nothing. But the spirit of God moving in and through you is invincible; it is all-powerful. That spirit is represented by the word, "I".

The personal "I" is the ego, the part of us that believes in lies and limitation. The impersonal or spiritual "I" is infinite with unlimited potential. There is only One True "I" and that is God. When you realize that this is the real power behind "I can," you increase your ability to achieve.   You release limitation. You get the entire

To educate the heart, one must be willing to go out of himself, and to come into loving contact with others.

-- -- *Unknown*

responsibility for achievement off your back and put it squarely on God where it belongs.

Through God, in you, you have the power to accomplish the seemingly impossible. That is why you can declare with power and authority, "I can!" The best part is that you can let go of the need to work excessively to *make* something happen.

Achievement becomes more difficult for people who mistakenly believe they must work hard as though it all depends on them. While your effort (sometimes a lot of it) is required, you have vast unlimited power within you. Nothing would ever be accomplished without it. Nothing! Remember the lilies, neither do they spin or toil, yet nothing is arrayed such as these. (Matt. 6: 28-29) They make no effort. They just know that by their very existence, by being what they are, their beauty will manifest.

Take a little time and visit your flower garden, if you have one, or visit a neighbor's garden. Pick out a flower, such as a beautiful rose. Look at it from the ground up and take note of what you see. From outward appearances, the rose is doing nothing, but within the rose—within the bush and each flower—the substance of God is at work. (Or if you have a lawn, you might sit

*I am not discouraged, because
every wrong attempt discarded
is another step forward.*
-- Thomas A. Edison

and watch the grass grow—though sooner or later you're going to have to mow it! Forgive the stark reminder, but with all its effortless ability to be grass, unfortunately, it can't mow itself.) The point is, as it is within the rose, it is within you and me.

The second word of the phrase—the word "can"—contains the faith to move mountains. It is the moving force that produces results. When you declare "I can"—remembering that "I" stands for The One, and "can" stands for the moving power of that One—you get yourself out of the way and the whole universe comes to fulfill your desire. It is such an ingenious arrangement, only God could have thought it up. The best part is, He gave it to you and me and everyone, as a gift. *Thank You, God!*

I don't know if Jesus Christ gave much conscious thought to the seemingly miraculous things he did, but he certainly had the "I can" attitude. To Him, it was natural. But it should be remembered that He said, "The things I do, you can do, and greater things." He was saying, in effect, that He was no different from you and me—that we all have the same power to do great things through the speaking of our word. And when our "word" is, "I can," things are going to happen! It is just as natural to us as it was to Jesus Christ

We are what we think.
All that we are arises
With our thoughts,
We make our world.
          -- The Buddha

Michelangelo, who could "see" the finished statue in a block of marble, knew he could bring it out for all to see. A baby who sees other people walking, and hears them talking, somehow believes, "I can do that, too!" We've all been there and done that.

There is a basic universal law that like attracts like; what you give out is what you get back—multiplied. When you apply the principle of "I can," keeping in mind the universal law, you will not fail to bring to yourself the kind of happiness and fulfillment you only dreamed of before. By blessing yourself, in an unseen way, you help to bless everyone else, because we are all one..

*Anytime you have difficulty making
an important decision, you can
be sure that it's the result of
being unclear about your values.*
-- Anthony Robbins*

3

The "Eye Can"

Now it's time to make your "Eye CAN." Making your Eye CAN is fun and easy. Be sure to make your own can, rather than using one someone else has made for you. It is okay to assist children in making their Eye CANs, but it will appeal and mean more to them if you allow them to do as much as possible for themselves. Children *love* this idea, and so do adults!

1. Obtain any size metal can, preferably one with a paper label that can be removed.

2. Wash the can thoroughly, removing the label. You can, if you wish, wrap the can in plain white or colored paper.

3. Look through women's magazines for colorful pictures of eyes. (Make-up ads are the best.) An actual full-color photo is best. Do NOT use black and white photos. (See the picture on the cover of this book.)

*When written in Chinese,
the word "crisis" is composed
of two characters — one represents danger
and the other represents opportunity.*

— John F. Kennedy

4. When you have found the eye you want, neatly cut it out, including the eyebrow. It should be as realistic-looking as possible.

5. Using a glue stick or rubber cement, attach the eye to the outside of the can. Be sure to use enough glue so that the eye will stay attached to the surface.

6. Do nothing else to the can. Add no other decorations.

7. Place your new Eye CAN where you will see it easily (and where it will "see" you.)

Make several Eye CANs and place them in your office, bedroom, bathroom, living room, den, and other places. Put one on your television and in your car. One lady I know made a very small Eye CAN and put it in her purse. An artist who attended one of my classes, drew a very colorful eye and attached it to a five-gallon popcorn can, and presented it to me. It got everyone's attention!

Man is not the creature of circumstances;
circumstances are the creatures of men.
-- Benjamin Disraeli

4

Expect Something Good

When you make your Eye CAN, expect something good to happen. Just by making it, your spirits will begin to rise, and your expectations should rise, too! You are using a simple but dynamic idea to help build an inner-belief system, which, in turn, produces good results. Your Eye CAN will remind you that you truly can have everything. It will help you reach higher than ever before.

Many people practice a lot of denial, meaning that they deny much of the good that God is trying to give them. They hold negative beliefs that they are unworthy or incapable of achieving much more than what they've already experienced. They falsely believe that it is too much to expect to rise out of their self-imposed ruts and live more in keeping with the way God intends for them to live.

*Blessed is the person who is
too busy in the day time and too
sleepy to worry at night
-- Leo Aikman*

But you CAN attract to you all that will make you happy and your life complete. You can be blessed in every wonderful way. You can be healed, happy and prosperous. You can achieve things that might have seemed impossible before. You can be free from doubts, debts, worry, anxiety and fear. During our tenure here on Mother Earth, we have every right to claim and accept the abundant life we were assured was ours. We are here to live victorious and free.

Countless people have changed their lives for the better when they finally began to visualize that better life and say, "I can do that." And they went ahead and proved it to be true. What others have done, you can do. Even things no one has ever done, you can do. So go ahead and do it—after, of course, you have made your Eye CAN.

*Most of all, do not dwell on failure
or mistakes, and never feel guilty
about anything done or not done.*
           -- -- *John Wolcott Adams,*
                Thirty Days To a Better Life

5

What Do You Want?

Once you begin to embrace the idea that you CAN have everything, construct your Eye CAN to serve as a reminder, and expect good results, the next step is to do some exploring. Too often, people have only vague, undefined concepts of what they want, then wonder why they are unable to achieve satisfaction in life.

You can have everything, but what does *everything* mean to you? What is it that you really want? What will satisfy the longings of your heart? Love, peace of mind, success? Health, wealth, happiness, freedom? A college degree? A happy relationship with someone you love and who loves you? Your own business? Travel? To be a multimillionaire? To write a best-selling book? Something unique to you?

Think about the things you want. Write them down. Just be sure it is right, good and worthwhile—in accord with the law of divine love. And be sure to have an Eye CAN in sight wherever you go to write and review your goals.

If wisdom were offered me with the proviso that I should keep it shut up, and refrain from declaring it, I should refuse. There is no delight in owning anything unshared. -- Seneca

Imagination plays a big role in the demonstration of what you want to achieve. Take time to be still and "see" with your imagination. See yourself enjoying your heart's desires. When an artist paints a picture, he first sees the finished picture in his mind. Add feeling to what you see in your imagination, and your heart's desires cannot help but manifest for you.

Feeling, too, is essential for achieving. While it is powerful to speak affirmations and to declare, "I can," the real power lies in *feeling*. The power is *God in you*. So, when you see your Eye CAN "looking" at you, let it remind you to feel your oneness with God. The more you use your imagination and your "faith feeling," the happier and more fulfilled you will become.

When you hold in your mind an active, alive and clear picture of what you desire, and KNOW within yourself that is already yours, it's a done deal! Nothing can prevent it from coming to you.

*A pessimist is one who makes difficulties
of his opportunities.
An optimist is one who makes opportunities
of his difficulties.   -- John Ruskin*

6

"I Cans"

Write down some "I Cans" to assist you in doing more, believing more, achieving more and, at the same time, helping everyone around you to be happier, healthier, more harmonious and fulfilled. Place them inside your Eye CAN where you can pull them out whenever you need a reminder of the wealth of resources within you.

Here are some examples:

I Can make a difference in the world.
I Can contribute to . . .

> world peace.
> someone else's joy and happiness.

I Can be . . .

> Happy.
> Healthy.
> Loving.
> Kind.
> Considerate.

*Every situation -- nay, every moment --
is of infinite worth; for it is the
representative of a whole eternity.*
                                        -- Goethe

Friendly.
Gentle.
Caring.
Prosperous.
Successful.
Assertive.
Understanding.
I Can help someone . . .
I Can have what I want!

Now write your personal "I CAN" list.

I Can . . .

_____

_____

_____

_____

_____

_____

_____

_____

_____

_____

_____

_____

_____

To a dull mind all of nature is leadened.
To the illumined mind
the whole world sparkles with light.
-- Ralph Waldo Emerson

7

Beware the Power of Doubt and Fear

Many people fail in their quests for happy, fulfilling lives because of doubt and fear. They doubt themselves and fear to attempt. Doubt and fear often block their vision of the greater good the universe holds for them. Even if they are able to see it, their own negative belief systems can convince them that they really can't be successful, so they are afraid to make the effort.

But those who have utilized the Eye CAN have very easily overcome doubt and fear, and gone on to achieve more than they ever thought possible. A young man, who had doubted he could ever get to college, received a full scholarship—much to his surprise and delight. This simple, yet powerful tool will dissolve your doubt and fear, too, and give you the faith and confidence to achieve whatever you want. In reality, doubt and fear have only the power you choose to give them.

People fear to take action because of the opinions or anger of other people. Some people—even some

Thunder is good, thunder is impressive;
but it is the lightning that does the work.

-- Mark Twain

parents—use fear, anger, even money to dominate or control the people around them. This is wrong. I remember being afraid of what family members or other people would think or say about my ideas or actions, which were honorable most of the time (though I was known to be quite a mischief-maker in my early years).

Controlling people often are insecure. They doubt their own ability to meet certain tasks or to deal with other people. So they create a façade of anger, threats and fear to hide their own insecurity and maintain control.

Doubt and fear inhibit the flow of creativity. We are all creative. Our wonderful minds flow with unlimited ideas and potential. So many more ideas would be manifested if doubt and fear didn't block the flow.

The way to overcome doubt and fear is love. Love is the foundation of faith and the real power of achievement, the power that gives you the "I can" attitude for creating a safe, positive environment in which to thrive.

To overcome fear, face it. Life is full of challenges, some seemingly difficult. See your challenges for what they are—opportunities to draw upon your innate

I would rather be able to appreciate things I cannot have than to have things I cannot appreciate.
-- Elbert Hubbard

spiritual power. We all have vast reservoirs of spiritual potential waiting to be used. The right idea, the right person will show up just when needed. This happens to me all the time!

All you need to know is that you have everything you need to meet all challenges victoriously. The golden key is to not give doubt and fear any more power than they deserve, which is no power at all. When you cast doubt and fear aside, you *can* be successful.

*The highest reward for your toil
is not what you get for it,
but what you become by it.*
-- John Ruskin

8

Persist

Once you have made your Eye CAN, you should expect immediate results, because they are often very quick in coming. However, if your desired results seem to take a little longer, do not be dismayed. The longer it takes, the greater will be your demonstration. (Though don't put off accepting the good you desire just to try to make it larger!) Your Eye CAN will prove its value to you in amazing ways. No matter what the obstacles, the apparent delay, your Eye CAN will serve to remind you that you *can* and *will* achieve all that is truly important to you.

A successful businesswoman wrote her affirmations for achieving her goals, then put them inside her Eye CAN. Every day she took them out, read them and declared them. In an amazing way, this empowered her to achieve what she really wanted—and she wanted plenty! Her business and prosperity substantially improved. It was difficult for her to contain her joy—so she didn't try! (You can find more information on

Wise men appreciate the good of all men, for they see the good in each and know how hard it is to make anything good.   -- Baltasar Gracian

affirmations and the power of your spoken word in my book *Power Words for Prosperous Living!*, which contains more than 200 prospering affirmations.)

Do NOT be in a hurry. Hurry creates delay. Let your Eye CAN help you to confidently persist in the assurance that you will be successful. The more you use your Eye CAN, the more valuable and powerful it will be in your life.

Remember: our universe is teeming with every possibility. The universe wants to help you to be successful. It wants to give you ideas to make you rich and fulfilled. You can receive ideas by asking for them and listening within. When you receive them, put them to work.

Never be content with accepting only enough to get by. Anybody can do that. Do not accept the belief that you are meant to live any other way than in perfect health, with plenty of happiness, love, harmony, peace and, of course, money.

Remove the limits in your thinking and you remove the limits on yourself, your life and your achievements. Your innate power for achievement is boundless. *Persist!*

*Do the very best work possible
under whatever conditions and with
whatever tools are provided.
See the work as worthwhile.
Devote it to God. Fill it with love.
Appreciate the bad with the good.
Let your love and appreciation
flow to others.   -- Unknown*

9

The Lady and the Captain

This is the story of one woman who used her Eye CAN to achieve the life she wanted.

While I was working to establish the Unity church in Port Angeles, I taught a series of classes based on the book Psycho-Cybernetics, by the late Dr. Maxwell Maltz. Among my students was a woman with the most beautiful white hair—a really lovely lady. To look at her, no one would suspect that anything ever bothered her. However, one day after class, she asked to talk with me.

"Estelle" (not her real name) began to tell me about her husband. She told me he had become very difficult to live with and was making her life miserable.

For more than 20 years, "Charlie" had been a captain of a merchant ship. He had been retired for several years, but from what Estelle told me, it appeared that he still needed a ship to run and a crew to command. He would not let her do much of anything without

Getting an idea is like sitting down on a pin, it should make you jump up and do something! -- E. S. Simpson

complaint. Even more than complain, he made life so unpleasant for her, she would rather obey than live in disharmony.

She couldn't go to her doctor. She couldn't leave out in plain sight the metaphysical books she loved to read. "I can't go to my church, or have friends over," she said. "Relatives stay away. If they do visit, it isn't for long, because they feel so uncomfortable when my husband is at home. I even have to sneak out to attend your class. Usually I make up something so he won't know. He won't let me have a garden, let alone help me with one." She went on describing how cantankerous and unreasonable the old fellow had become.

As if that weren't bad enough, Charlie had a most unpleasant habit of greeting her at the breakfast table by saying: "I feel terrible, just rotten. I think I'm going to die today. I feel like it." *(Estelle probably had to restrain herself from wishing he would!)* When Charlie made his pronouncement, Estelle usually tried to console him, to make timid arguments against such a thing happening.

What a way to start the day! No one should be greeted in such a manner. As Estelle talked, it was amazing to watch her lovely countenance contort with hurt and frustration. Her eyes filled with tears as she

Genuine happiness comes through getting in touch with the real energy of right living conditions and activity. That energy is love, and love empowers you to live life lovingly, happily, and prosperously.

-- John Wolcott Adams

How to Have "Unexpected" Income

spoke of her husband. It pained her to talked that way about someone she loved, although she sometimes wondered whether she did love him anymore. She wanted to know what, if anything, could be done to change her circumstances, because she desperately desired to be free, to enjoy life. She longed for peace and harmony.

That day we prayed together. I gave her a couple of affirmations to use, and she left for home, feeling assured that, somehow, things would improve.

Throughout the following week, I kept Estelle in my thoughts and prayers. Something seemed to assure me that there was a really good solution for her problem, and that the solution was forthcoming, though I couldn't yet grasp what it was. I kept my mind open to guidance, to the right idea or solution for bringing peace and harmony into Estelle's and Charlie's home for the good of them both.

It is important to note here that the atmosphere that surrounds us all is permeated with ideas. When we listen and are receptive, they will reveal themselves to our minds. They will literally come alive in our thinking.

*You are born every time you breathe,
and you have lived forever.*
-- -- *Unknown*

I kept myself open, kept listening. Then one day, when I least expected it, the "light" came on! Estelle's words really stood out in my mind: "I can't." The problem was so obvious, I wondered why I hadn't realized it before. She had convinced herself she *couldn't* do certain things because of Charlie's nasty attitude and behavior. But it wasn't so much his behavior as it was her fear that created the problem. She had created, with his help, such a fearful feeling that she wouldn't do anything she thought might upset him.

In truth, another person can never dominate us unless we allow it. Each one of us holds the power over our own thinking, our own lives. *You can always choose to correct any situation.* That is the first step. The next step is to realize that you *can* do it.

The idea of the Eye CAN came into my mind. I had seen it work with teenagers and some other adults, and I felt assured it would work for her, even though it seemed such a simple solution for such a seemingly complex problem. But who ever said that solutions need to be complicated? I could hardly wait to share this idea with Estelle. After all, what did she have to lose but a lot of unhappiness?

The unforgivable sin is simply the closed mind that is made up, that will not let the Spirit reveal new Truths.

- - Eric Butterworth

When I arrived for our next class, Estelle was already there, waiting for me. She looked a little shocked when I repeated back to her all the "I can't" statements she had been making. I explained how she had created a belief system that so inhibited her, she actually believed she couldn't do the things she wanted to do. That pattern needed to be interrupted, I told her. It needed to be transformed into a "can do" pattern of thought that would create more positive actions, make her feel better about herself and her capabilities, and protect her from the blasts of negativity Charlie launched in her direction.

So I told her to make an Eye CAN. At that, Estelle looked at me as though I had lost my marbles. "An 'eye' can? What in the world is that?" she asked with surprise. So I showed her my own Eye CAN and explained that since I had seen it work so well before, I was sure it would work for her, too. After all, I told her, children love this idea, and as the Master-Teacher taught, if you really want satisfying results, "become as little children." Besides, simple methods are usually more effective than complicated ones where precious time is wasted just trying to figure out how to make them work. And the Eye CAN was about as simple as they come—*really lo-tech!*

Love never leaves you where it finds you . . . even as it approves of you, it improves you.   - - J. Stig Paulson

The Eye CAN, I explained, was designed simply to remind her to keep telling herself, "I can" rather than "I can't." Whenever she looked at the can, she would be reminded that she really could do anything she genuinely wanted to do. I told her to place her Eye CAN in a conspicuous place where she could see it (and it could "see" her). Whenever she found her thoughts focusing on things she couldn't do, she was to affirm instead, "I can." She was to affirm this only to herself, saying nothing to Charlie or to anyone.

By now, she was beginning to smile and get excited about making her own Eye CAN. She agreed she would make one as soon as she got home.

But before we ended our discussion, I addressed the subject of Charlie's dire breakfast table predictions. I suggested that the next time he came to the breakfast table and uttered his statements about dying, she should simply "agree" with him. "Oh, but I can't do that," she said. "I'd be afraid of what he might do." I gently reminded her that if she was to improve her life, that old "I can't" habit of thinking had to be discarded. She agreed to somehow find the courage to try.

At class the next week, Estelle told me she had made her Eye CAN and placed it on the window ledge

Love is like Rhubarb. The more love is divided and expressed the more it grows, not only in quantity but in beauty and tenderness as well. -- Dale Batesole

above the kitchen sink where she could easily see it. Every time she went near it, she told me, it seemed to be looking at her, reminding her that she really could do whatever she put her mind to. Something in her voice and in the look on her face told me that something was stirring inside her. She said she had been feeling better. Nothing in particular had happened yet, and Charlie hadn't discovered the can on the ledge. After all, he never helped with the dishes.

The following week, Estelle met me at class, fairly bubbling over with excitement. She could hardly contain her joy as she described how she had gained new courage. The old doubts and fears were dissolving, and the faith she thought had deserted her had returned, stronger than ever.

She said she had made up her mind to do things she previously had believed she couldn't. She would go to her doctor if necessary. She would leave her books where they would be handy and no longer make any pretense about attending my classes.

Then her eyes lit up as she told me that one morning, not long after she had made her Eye CAN, her courage peaked as Charlie came to the breakfast table. This time she was ready for him. Like an old

The thing always happens that you believe in; and the belief in a thing makes it happen.

-- Frank Lloyd Wright

record he groaned with even more certainty in his voice. "I feel terrible, just awful. I'm sure I'm going to die today. Oh-h-h."

Looking right at him, and without hesitation, she smiled and said, "Well that's just fine, dear. You go right ahead if that's what you want to do. It's really a good day for it."

At first, there was silence. Charlie looked blank as his wife's words began to sink in. She had never said anything like that to him before. He liked Estelle to be agreeable, but this was entirely too much! A look of astonishment came over him. How could this woman, whom he had dominated for so long, agree that he might just as well die and do it that day?

Then the unexpected happened. Charlie leaned back in his chair so far that he almost toppled over backwards! He roared with laughter. It was the first time in years Estelle had heard him laugh like that.

She went on to say that, though only a few days had passed, Charlie hadn't mentioned dying since. Harmony was beginning to gain a foothold in their home.

The real payoff came when she returned home

Desire is the springboard to all achievement; the foundation on which goal realization is based. Anythng that is truly desired is ultimately possible to achieve.
- - *Dr. James E. Melton,*
Vital Enthusiasm

from class one day to find Charlie out in the yard, preparing the ground for a garden for her.

Months later, when I saw Estelle again, she seemed better looking than ever. "I can't thank you enough," she said, and added that she still kept her Eye CAN on the window ledge. With a radiant smile, she told me how pleasant Charlie had become. "We've become good friends," she said. Charlie was still trying to figure out what had come over *her*, but by now, Estelle was not the only one who had changed inside.

Neighbors, relatives and friends couldn't believe the difference in Charlie. They were delighted to find him to be a most charming and helpful man, a great story teller who had found new joy in opening up to people and sharing some of his experiences at sea. In addition, Charlie evidently realized he had a jewel of a wife and, in his own way, decided to appreciate her for as long as he could. It appeared he had finally retired from the ship, and that was fine with Estelle. "Now," she said, "life is wonderful!"

When we love enough, we see correctly with an illumined vision. The golden key is in focusing our attention upon love. Love is the golden answer to everything. Love is life and what you are.

-- John Wolcott Adams,
Be What You Are: Love

10

A Real Estate Salesman
Makes the "Impossible" Sale

I was teaching another class, this time in the small desert community of El Centro, California, when I met "George", a real estate salesman. George had an exciting, prospering experience that made him a believer in the power of the Eye CAN.

By the second class, as instructed, George and the other members of the class had constructed their own Eye CANs. As the weeks passed, students began reporting some relatively small events that had occurred. One woman had gained more than five pounds over the Christmas holidays, but had put off doing anything about it because she believed it would be too difficult. After making her Eye CAN, she changed her attitude. She reassessed her eating and exercise habits, and reported to the class that she had already shed two pounds. One man in the class improved his golf game after making his Eye CAN.

You have a master purpose in life, and that is to be your Self --- the Self you are created to be. -- J. Sig Paulson

Then one day, George announced that he could hardly wait for me to ask for reports. His excitement was obvious. So when I asked for reports, he sprang to his feet and, with great enthusiasm, began telling everyone about the events of the past week.

It seems that in the Imperial Valley, one of the best farming areas of California, the farms are quite large. George reported that he had received a call from the owner of one of the larger farms, telling him that he would like to sell his farm. George knew another party who was interested in buying that particular farm. From all appearances, he said, it looked like an easy sale that would reward him with an extra-large commission check.

However, when his broker learned of the deal, he informed George that the farm could not be sold because the owner had recently given a three-year lease to someone else. He told George, "There is no way that property can change hands now, so you may as well forget it."

You can just imagine the *deflation* of George's elation. He sank back into his chair as a cloud of disappointment came over him. He sat there for a long time, thinking. He thought of the other people involved— of *their* disappointment. Even the thought of that nice

*No life grows great until it is
focused, dedicated and disciplined.
-- Harry Emerson Fosdick*

commission passed through his mind, the way that sale had seemingly passed through his fingers. He decided he'd better let the deal go and get to work on something else.

Then he spotted his Eye CAN, next to the phone on his desk. It seemed to be looking right at him as if to say, "Why do you just sit there? YOU *CAN* SELL THAT PROPERTY. YOU'D BETTER BELIEVE IT!"

"But how?" he thought. Then, George said, he almost shouted the words, "I can!"

"Some way, somehow," he thought, "I *can* sell that farm!"

George became very quiet as he began to search for answers. He had long been a student of the Power of the Mind, and knew the power of thinking in the right direction. So George began to focus his thoughts—his Mind-Power—on what he wanted to achieve, knowing that, if at all possible, the desired results would manifest. This is one of the success secrets of the Eye CAN.

George kept saying to himself, "I can! I can! I can sell that property! There is a way. I *know* it." Again he looked at his Eye CAN, and then came the light!

*Neither a lofty degree of intelligence
nor imagination nor both together
go to the making of genius.
Love, love, love, that is the soul of genius.*
— *Mozart*

At once he reached for the phone and called the party who had leased the farm from the owner. George explained the situation and, to his surprise, learned that the man no longer wanted to farm that place, because property had been made available to him in the area he desired to live, northern California. He didn't know how to get out of the lease without penalty, so he had assumed he wouldn't be able to take advantage of that opportunity.

George then put in a call to the farm owner. After some negotiation, and to George's delight, the owner agreed to let the fellow out of the lease without penalty so that the sale could go through. Arrangements were made to get all the parties together, and the deal was finalized. The owner received what he wanted, and the buyer was satisfied with the price. The man leasing the property was happy, too, given up to a month to vacate the property. The papers were drawn up and signed.

George was delighted to see so many happy people, but his delight grew to joy when he received his commission check!

What made him most happy, however, was the ease with which the Eye CAN worked for him. It helped him to overcome disappointment and to draw on his

True preparation for wealth is in the mind.
Ideas are the coin of the mind realm.
Make of your mind
the abiding place of rich thought.
— Ernest Wilson

unlimited Mind-Power for success.

You can be sure, George remains a strong believer in the Eye CAN idea, and has gone on to achieve other prospering results. Several months after his big sale, he wrote to tell me he had purchased income property, become a broker, and established himself in his own real estate office. He was able to achieve all this, he wrote, because he had first written down his goals, then used the Eye CAN in conjunction with goal-setting, meditation and other methods he had learned. He wrote that he had achieved his goals more than a year ahead of schedule. *It works!*

*Sense of inferiorty can be conquered
only through the daily overcoming of
small obstacles.
As we take on larger tasks eventually
we reach the sense of achievement and
growth that is self-confidence.
God has a plan for every life.
Earnest seeking has never failed to
find the true trail.*

-- -- Melvin J. Evans

11

It Can Happen To You!

Amazing things happen when you dare to get definite about your desires, write them down on paper, and make an Eye CAN. When you make yours, and place it where you can easily see it, it will remind you, "I can have anything . . . everything my heart desires."

As it has worked for the people you've met in this book, it will work for you, and in any situation. In every case, the principle is the same: you CAN ACHIEVE whatever you BELIEVE you can. The Eye CAN helps you in a silent, but powerful way to create within yourself a vital, alive, positive and victorious success attitude for productive results—a true, empowering belief system. You cannot fail and you *know* it. You know you have all the resources of the universe available to you, within you. You know you can have all that you deeply desire. Make your own Eye CAN and prove it for yourself.

Believe you can, and you can;
believe you will, and you will.
See yourself achieving, and you will achieve.
Never give up; giving up is like letting
go of a life preserver when you
are almost saved.
You cannot lose if you hang on.
        - - Gardner Hunting

A promising young female athlete suffered a severe injury in a fall, which left her partially paralyzed. When doctors said she would never walk again, she refused to believe it. She said, with great conviction and knowing, "I CAN AND I WILL WALK AGAIN! I WILL BE COMPLETELY HEALED." She not only walked, she was healed.

Among my former students were a postmaster and his wife. The postmaster once wrote to me from Hawaii, explaining that he and his wife were on their way to the Orient. It was a trip they had dreamed of for years, but things didn't come together until they attended my classes and made their Eye CANs. He wrote that he finally realized that he actually *could* fulfill his long-held desire to take his wife to the Orient, and the trip had come about only a few months after making their Eye CANs.

The "impossible" is always possible. I sometimes look back at the accomplishments I've made by simply believing "I can," then backing up my belief with positive action in line with my goals. I say this humbly, because I know that, of myself, I can do nothing, but the infinite Mind-Power within me is capable of doing whatever it is aimed toward. It is invincible, all-conquering.

*Whatever you ask in prayer, believe
that you receive it, and you will.*
-- *Mark 11:24*

I am grateful for my understanding of this. With it, I was able to create a new church in a small city. In addition, I began the Golden Key Ministry—a worldwide prayer ministry by mail—with nothing more than an idea, an old mechanical typewriter (one of those green-keyed Royal Standards that some of you may remember), my kitchen table, a small mailing list, and very little money. But I had my goals, my faith, and my Eye CAN.

In spite of its meager beginning, the Golden Key Ministry continues to grow. It is rewarding to know that it is now serving the spiritual needs of numerous people in many parts of the world.* I now have my faithful computer and other office equipment to make the work easier. With dedicated prayer partners who work with me, the ministry continues to support people in prayer wherever they are.

*We cannot experience the abundance
of God until we have conquered
our self-imposed limitations.
We cannot fill our cups to overflowing
with the eternal riches of Spirit
when the capacity of our cups is restricted
by the sediment of self-defeating
concepts and habits.*

-- -- *Ernest Holmes*

12

Action – Your Golden Key to Results

Now that you know what to do, do it! As wonderful and helpful as your Eye CAN will prove to be, do not be fooled into thinking that all you have to do is make one. Take action toward what you want to achieve, and results will be automatic. Do everything you can to help make your dreams come true.

Believe you will receive. Back up your belief with action, and every action with belief. Declare often: "I can! I CAN! I *can* achieve, because I *believe* I can! With God's help, I can, and I am!" The mark of success is upon you! You were born with it and it has never left you.

It is my pleasure to share these ideas with you. Please write and let me know the results of your Eye CAN. I will immensely appreciate hearing from you. Now have fun with your Eye CAN and enjoy your healthier, happier, more fulfilling life.

John Wolcott Adams
P.O. Box 30989. Phoenix, AZ 85046-0989 USA

If you don't like <u>where</u> you are change <u>what</u> you are.
-- Henry Knight Miller

This habit of expectancy always marks a strong person. It is a form of attraction: our own comes to us because we desire it. We find what we expect to find, and we receive what we ask for.
-- Elbert Hubbard

Positive Prayers

I CAN do all things through
the power of God in me.

I CAN have all the desires
of my heart now.

I CAN Have Everything!

All doors are open!
All channles are free!
And, God now gives
His best to me!

At Poverty Station, I just scoff--
I go right on by, but don't get off.
With Abundance as my rightful ration,
Prosperity Station is my Destination!

*God's love brings forth the
fulfillment of all your needs.
There is nothing that
His love cannot fulfill.*
       *-- John Wolcott Adams,
          "Positively Alive!"*

More Positive Prayers

I Can do, be, have,
whatever I really desire.

With a thankful heart, I am
open and receptive to all the
good God has for me.

Drawing upon the unlimited
Power within me, I know
I CAN do anything.

I CAN live victoriously, happy,
healthy, peaceful, prosperous
and free, and I AM.

I CAN make a positive difference
in other people's lives, and I AM.

*God's love brings forth the
fulfillment of all your needs.
There is nothing that
His love cannot fulfill.*
   *-- John Wolcott Adams,
      "Positively Alive!"*

Notes

Record of I CAN happenings

Enjoy all of John Wolcott Adams' books.

Positively Alive!
Thirty Days To A Better Life
Power Words For Prosperous Living!
BE What You Are: LOVE
How To Have 'Unexpected' Income!
How I CAN Have Everything!
Pro$per Now!
Life Is Choice
(Please use the order form on page 101)

Positively Alive! This book is full of inspiration, ideas, and guidance for healthy, happy, wealthy, peaceful and positive living everyday. You will find answers to life's daily challenges in this book. It will lift your faith and give you the power to live more creatively, lovingly, successfully, and prosperously. Some of the chapter titles are: Today Is A New Beginning; Inner Strength; No Difficulty Is Beyond Solution; Claim Your Freedom Now, When Things Look The Worst, Put Yourself Up.

BE What You Are: LOVE! This inspiring book teaches you how to experience true health and happiness, peace and prosperity, and miracles! It gives you the Golden Key to freedom from fear, to make your life worthwhile, and your dreams come true! This book

Filling yourself and your home with love creates a force field of irresistible prospering energy that literally magnetizes more and more good to you.
-- John Wolcott Adams,
Be What You Are: Love

empowers you to be what you truly are. Chapter titles include: Sufficient Love Will Do It, Love Is Freedom From Fear, More Prosperity In Your Home, Love is Life!

Power Words For Prosperous Living! Would you like to live a more positive, affirmative and prosperous way of life? This book teaches you how. A must read book to help you live prosperously and successfully without the usual struggle and strain. It contains over 200 of the most powerful prosperity affirmations you. would ever dare to use. A few the chapter titles are: Your Spoken Word Is Power!, It's Right To Be Rich!, Your "Divine Connection," How To Use Power Words for Prosprously Living. An excellent companion to the next book.

How To Have 'Unexpected' Income! This is a very popular book and for good reason. It gives you usable ideas which you can put to work now to increase your prosperity. This book is the culmination of many years of helping thousands of happy people to prosper through learning *How To Have 'Unexpected' Income.* It makes prosperity more fun, too! Chapter titles include: You Can Cause a Flow of Financial Abundance in Your Life, Prayer-Treatment for 'Unexpected' Income, The "Gratitude Attitude," plus, numerous testimonials.

A self confident attitude is the most important asset a person can possess.
-- Andrew Carnegie

Thirty Days To A Better Life! This small but mighty book will guide you to achieve all that is really important to

you. It helps you weed out the unessentials and to focus the great energy of your mind on what you really want, and helps you get it! *Thirty Days To A Better Life* will help make your dreams come true -- much more quickly! A few chapters are: You Deserve The Best!, There Is A Way, You Can Have It All!!, The Mark of Success Is Upon You!   A jewel of a book!

Pro$per Now! - 120 Dynamic Daily Inspirations to help you prosper. Why wait? This prosperity-power-packed book helps you to live more prosperously now. It covers every aspect of the Prosperous Life and gives you inspiration and ideas to help you stay on the prosperity path. If you love prosperity, and want more of it, this book is for you. Read daily and You will *Prosper Now!*

Life Is Choice - From A to Z, life is choice. You make numerous choices every day. This book is a treasure of positive help in making wise, loving, and positive choices for health and happiness, success and prosperity -- inspiration to start the day and positive ideas along the way. As with all of the author's books, this one is a wonderful book for gift-giving. *(Due out, late 2003*

*Nothing splendid has ever been
achieved except by those who dared to
believe that something inside them
was superior to circumstances.*

~ ~ Bruce Barton

You CAN do more than you might have believed you could. You can be happier, healthier, and wealthier because you have within you that which is invincible, all-conquering, and all-providing.. When you tap into this mighty resource and let it move in you and through you as it wants to, you will be amazed at what can be accomplished through you.

While the Great Force in you does the work, it's okay for you to take credit for what is done. Just remember to quietly thank the Source. You simply cannot deplete this magnificent power, so go ahead and *be* the instrument through which great things are achieved. You *can* when you believe you can!

- - John Wolcott Adams

Action seems to follow feeling, but really action and feeling go together; and by regulating the action, which is under the more direct control of the will, we can indirectly regulate the feeling, which is not.　- - Wm. James

Use this form to order the author's books

_____ *Positively Alive!* - $10.95

_____ *BE What You Are: LOVE!* - $8.95

_____ *Power Words For Prosperous Living!* - $8.95

_____ *How To Have 'Unexpected' Income!* - $8.95

_____ *Thirty Days To A Better Life!* - $5.95

_____ *How I CAN Have Everything!* - $12.95

_____ *Pro$per Now!* - $14.95

_____ *Life Is Choice* - $14.95   *(late 2003)*

Purchase these books where you bought this one,
or order directly from the author.

Order 10 or more copies of any of these titles (mix or match) and deduct 20% from your order. Prices in US dollars & include postage except Canada, Mexico & Overseas, please add 40% to total cost.

Send your order to: John Wolcott Adams

P. O. Box 30989, Phoenix, AZ 85046-0989

Credit Card orders: **www.GoldenKeyMinistry.com**

Name_____

Address_____

City, State, ZIP_____

Total amount enclosed: $_____

Contribution to Golden Key Ministry: $_____

Please mention the title of this book. (You may photocopy this page.)